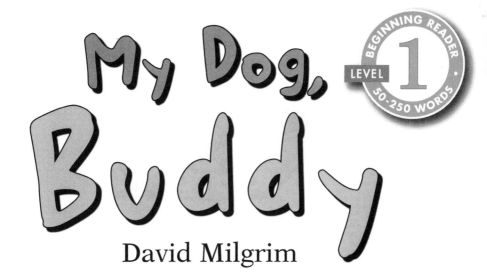

My Dog, Buddy

David Milgrim

BEGINNING READER
LEVEL 1
50-250 WORDS

Cartwheel
·B·O·O·K·S·®

SCHOLASTIC INC.
New York Toronto London Auckland Sydney
Mexico City New Delhi Hong Kong Buenos Aires

For Grandpa Ange

Copyright © 2008 by David Milgrim.

All rights reserved. Published by Scholastic Inc.
SCHOLASTIC, CARTWHEEL BOOKS, and associated logos
are trademarks and/or registered trademarks of Scholastic Inc.
Lexile is a registered trademark of MetaMetrics, Inc.

Library of Congress Cataloging-in-Publication Data
Milgrim, David.
My dog, Buddy / David Milgrim.
p. cm.
"Cartwheel books."
Summary: Mom, Dad, and brother Pete all try to get Buddy to obey,
but there is only one person in the family who knows how to communicate
with his mischievous canine friend.
ISBN-13: 978-0-545-03593-4
ISBN-10: 0-545-03593-7
[1. Dogs--Training--Fiction. 2. Human-animal relationships--Fiction.
3. Family life--Fiction.] I. Title.

PZ7.M5955My 2008
[E]--dc22   2007022795

ISBN-13: 978-0-545-03593-4
ISBN-10: 0-545-03593-7
10 9 8 7 6 5 4 3 2   8 9 10 11 12

Printed in the U.S.A. • First printing, September 2008

This is Buddy.

Dad tells Buddy
to sit.

Buddy stands up
and barks.

Dad tells him to stand up and bark.

Buddy sits.

Dad tells him
to come.

Buddy goes.

I tell Buddy to come.
Buddy comes.

Mom tells Buddy
to get the ball.

Buddy takes a nap.

Mom tells him
to get the paper.

Buddy rips it
to bits.

Mom says,
"STOP, STOP, STOP!"

Buddy goes, goes, goes.

I ask for a kiss.
Buddy gives me ten.

You have to know
how to talk to a dog.

One day, my brother, Pete,
told Buddy to roll over.

Buddy took his shoe
and ran away.

Buddy ran down the road.

He ran into Ms. Crum's house.

He ran
all the way
to the park.

Mom called.
Dad called.
Pete called.

But Buddy did not come.
Then they all looked at me.

I called, too.
And Buddy came!
I knew he would.

Buddy will do whatever you say.

You just need to know how to ask.

The
End